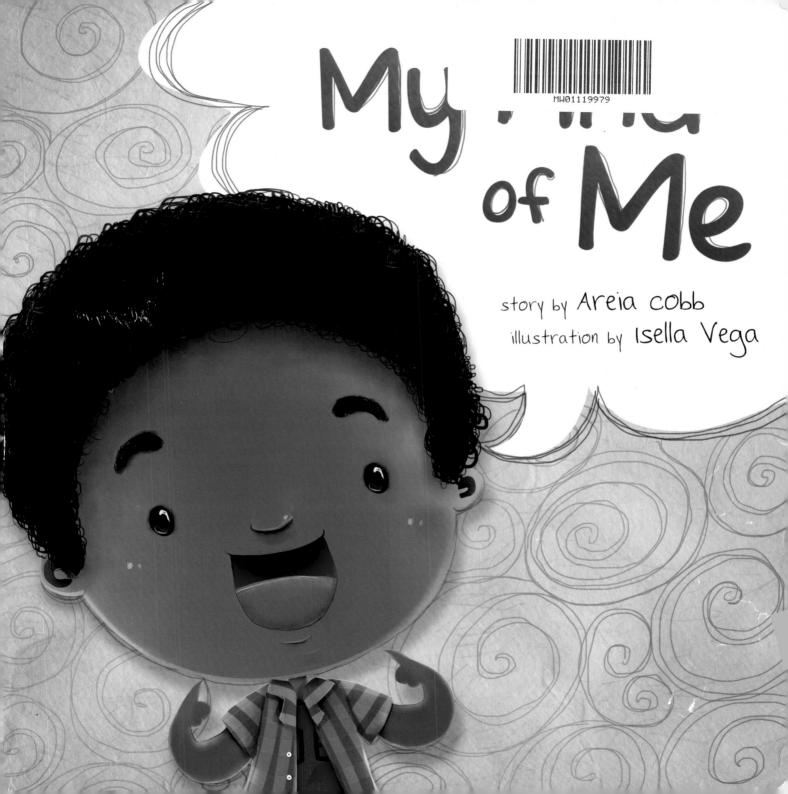

# My Kind of Me

story by Areia Cobb

illustration by Isella Vega

Published by Purpose Publishing
1503 Main Street #168 ❧ Grandview, Missouri
www.purposepublishing.com

ISBN: 978-0-9828379-8-6

Copyright © 2012, Areia Cobb

Illustrations and Cover design by: Isella Vega
Editing by: Millicent Connor

Printed in the United States of America

This book, or parts thereof, may not be reproduced, stored in a retrieval
system, or transmitted in any form or by means–
electronic, mechanical, photocopy, recording, or any other without
the prior permission of the publisher.

Inquiries may be addressed to:
info@acbookstore.net
www.acbookstore.net

This book is available at quantity discounts for bulk purchases.
For more information contact, www.acbookstore.net.

## Dedication

This is dedicated to anyone who has ever been made fun of for being themselves!

While Mrs. Jones class was outside for recess,
Langston noticed the new boy sitting by the trees all alone.
Since everyone else was running and playing,
Langston couldn't help but wonder if something was wrong.

"What's up dude, why are you sitting by yourself,
instead of running and playing with everybody else?"

"I tried that already, but it didn't work for me.
The other kids around don't seem to like what they see."

"They say I dress different and my hair is funny.
They also call me a teacher's pet for helping in class,
and say that I'm a nerd because I like Math.
It really hurts my feelings and sometimes I get mad,
but I don't know how to fight and snappy comebacks
I don't have."

"Have you ever told the teacher or even your mom and dad, that at school the kids pick on you, and it really makes you sad?"

"I thought about saying something,
but didn't want to add tattletale to my list of
names, so I'll just hang out with Mr. Tree,
while everyone else is playing games."

"Do you like the way you dress?
Do you like your hair?
Do you think that helping in class makes
you a square?"

"And so what you like
Math, numbers are cool.
Besides, learning is the
reason why you're in
school."

"Don't let others make you feel bad about being the person you want to be, as long as when you look in the mirror you like what you see."

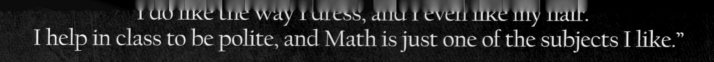

I do like the way I dress, and I even like my hair.
I help in class to be polite, and Math is just one of the subjects I like."

"Then again I ask why are you sitting under the tree.
You should enjoy being you, the way I enjoy being me."

"I thought I was ok until kids started calling me names.
Then I started to believe all the stuff that they were saying."

"It doesn't bother you when they call you names?
You don't wonder if you're too plain and try to change?"

"Listen, what's cool today won't be cool tomorrow,
but you will still be you, and that's what you have to learn
to accept. Being ok in your skin is the first step
to not trying to fit in.
Don't let what others think make you want to change
who you are. Being different is a gift.
Being unique makes you a star."

"I never thought of it that way."

"Whenever someone says something about me that used to hurt
my feelings I just say, I do what I do because I am who I am.
I don't wish to be you, because I like who I be.
I don't mean to be rude, but whether you agree or disagree;
it's simple to see....."

# I'M MY KIND OF ME !!

## Areia asks...

Have you ever been made fun of? Have you ever felt like you were an outcast because you dress, look or act different? I want to teach you that being different is not a bad thing. It is ok to have your own sense of style and to do things you find fun and interesting, even if the next kid thinks they are stupid. Often times people make fun of what they don't understand, because it's easier than admitting that they are different too.

## Langston says...

Realize that your uniqueness is the gift that makes you who you are, so don't stop being you in order to fit in. Learn to love who you are and you'll enjoy being your kind of you, the way I enjoy being My Kind of Me!

## Synopsis

It appears to me that people are most affected by what others think of them when they lack self-identity. *My Kind of Me* is meant to inspire self-love, and challenge children to accept themselves no matter what others think or say. I want young people to realize that what's cool today may not fit into who they are as individuals. So, instead of trying to fit into today's trend, create your own and stick to it because it's what you like. Styles and fads will come and go, but at the end of an era you will still be you. Do you like what you see?

## MY KIND OF ME...YOUR KIND OF YOU...Q & A

1. If someone hurts you with their hands or words, is it ok to keep it to yourself? (No)

2. Who should you tell if someone is picking on you? (Parents and Teachers)

3. No matter what others think you should always _ yourself? (Love)

4. Some people are afraid to be themselves, but you know that being _ is a gift. (Unique)

5. Is it ok to pick on someone just because everyone else is doing it? (No)

# My Kind of Me Crossword Puzzle

**Across**
2. Main Character
3. Who should you tell if someone picks on you
5. Being ? is a gift
6. Who should you tell if someone picks on you
7. It's ok to be
8. Subject the boy liked
9. Title of the book

**Down**
1. It takes ? to be different
2. Always ? yourself
4. Name the boy did not want to be called

**Word Bank:**
Langston, Different, My Kind of Me, Love, Math, Unique, Parents, Courage, Tattletale, Teacher

# My Kind of Me Word Search

```
E R O L I T A I A Q O L U N T
H L J Q U P S K Y T L U O P N
S T A T E A C H E R S T M A E
E E A T X Y U Z J T S N J R R
F T J M E N C J T G Q G I E E
J O L V I L Q O N T F W W N F
H C H Q U E T A U T O H T T F
B T U R E H L T O R Z J R S I
Y E R Y B S P P A C A Q X U D
L K S J C H M W M T V G C Q G
O B E V O L O O O N W R E Q K
B Q E Y N J Y Y U W M F Q V L
C Z G H L G O I V A V U R V K
K G F E M F O D N I K Y M L B
F Z F Q A Z C M E T I O Y R N
```

COURAGE
LANGSTON
MATH
PARENTS
TEACHERS

DIFFERENT
LOVE
MY KIND OF ME
TATTLETALE
UNIQUE

# ACKNOWLEDGEMENTS

**God you are so AWESOME!** Thank you for your inspiration, the talent you gifted me with and patience as I work daily to be the woman you want me to be.

**Family** – Thanks to all who believed in me to be and do something special from day one. And special thanks to those who stayed on me to pick up my pen and get back to work.

**Kevin and Langston** - You two are the reason I work so hard to be everything you both need me to be. Your love and support mean more than I could ever express.

# ABOUT THE AUTHOR

Born in Kansas City, KS on May 7, 1978, Areia grew up in Kansas City, MO where she lived until she was 18. Always told that she would be something special, she believed in herself at a very young age. Whether it was being active in church, taking pictures for the school yearbook, or writing poetry and short stories in her spare time, Areia made a point to utilize her gifts at every chance. After becoming a published poet in high school she knew that writing was what she wanted to do more than anything. This inspired her move to Atlanta, GA to attain a B.A. in Mass Media Arts – Radio/T.V./Film from Morris Brown College.

Continuing to write on and off, Areia's focus shifted to getting a 9-5 and as life took its course writing became something that she did less and less. After attaining a MBA, a job at her company of choice, getting married and having a child, Areia started back writing more frequently. Great ideas would come, but the works would never be completed. And then it happened...

One Monday in March 2012 as Areia was leaving work, the Holy Spirit spoke to her and told her to write this down. Immediately opening the notes APP in her iPhone she typed what she heard word for word. Once finished, Areia knew that was the theme of her first children's book. Two days later Areia prayed, "Lord, if this is for me, please reveal the remainder of the book today." He did just that... Later that day Areia started and completed her first book! Amazed at the timing and remembering her niece's dream about her writing a children's book, Areia quickly emailed the manuscript to her sister who forwarded to her Publisher friend.

Since that day, the ideas for My Kind of Me and other books have not stopped flowing. In fact, the following month Areia completed two more pieces, The Secret Inside and Real Imagination within hours of each other. Having so many incomplete works, Areia is certain that these books have been ordained by God and their purpose will be fulfilled.